Baby Says "Moo!"

WRITTEN BY JoAnn Early Macken

ILLUSTRATED BY David Walker

Disney • Hyperion Books

New York

Published by Disney · Hyperion Books, an imprint of Disney Book Group.

For information address Disney · Hyperion Books,

114 Fifth Avenue, New York, New York 10011-5690

First Edition

10 9 8 7 6 5 4 3 2 1

F850-6835-5-10319

Printed in Singapore · Reinforced binding

Designed by Scott Piehl

The type was set in Carrotflower.

The art was created by hand, using acrylic paint on paper.

Library of Congress Cataloging-in-Publication Data on file.

ISBN 978-1-4231-3400-8

Visit www.hyperionbooksforchildren.com

For the whole Macken clan, especially the babies

—J.E.M.

Especially for Charlie and Joe

—D.W.

Baby rolls along,
grabs a yummy snack,

waves at the people,
and they all wave back.

Baby, what do people say?
Baby says, "Moo!"

People say moo?
That can't be so.
Everybody knows that
people say hello.

A cow says moo,
sure as you're my bunny.
Where'd you ever find
an idea so funny?

Baby takes a ride
through the busy, dizzy city,

waves at a yellow bird
singing so pretty.

Baby, what do birds say?
Baby says, "Moo!"

A bird says moo?
Well, isn't that sweet?
But everybody knows that
a bird says tweet.

People say hello,
and a cow says moo,
sure as we will always be
me and you.

Baby zooms away.
Wheee! What fun!

Waves at a striped cat
stretching in the sun.

Baby, what do cats say?
Baby says, "Moo!"

A cat says moo?
I can't see how.
Everybody knows that
a cat says meow.

A bird says tweet,
and people say hello.

A cow says moo,
everywhere you go.

Baby cruises on,
smiling all the way,

waves at a horse
with its mouth full of hay.

Baby, what do horses say?
Baby says, "Moo!"

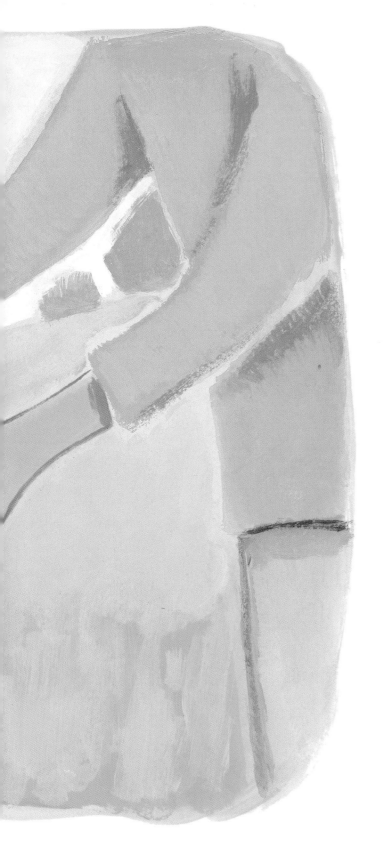

A horse says moo?
I have to say
everybody knows that
a horse says neigh.

 A cat says meow,
and a bird says tweet.

People say hello
when they pass
on the street.

A cow says moo
as it chomps and chews.
Sure as you're my lucky duck,
no one else moos.

Baby takes a stroll
down the hiking trail,

waves at a brown dog
wagging its tail.

Baby, what do dogs say?
Baby says, "Moo!"

A dog says moo?
What silly stuff!
Everybody knows that
a dog says ruff.

Out in the country
on a sunny summer day,
a prancing horse
says neigh, neigh, neigh.

 A cat says meow,
and a bird says tweet.

People say hello
to everyone they meet.

Isn't that true?
A cow says moo,

sure as you're my lovey-dove,
and I'm yours, too.

Look! There's an animal,
white and black.

A cow! A cow
with spots on its back!

What does Baby say?
Not one peep.

Tuckered-out Baby
is fast asleep.

Wake up, Baby! Here's a cow for you!

Baby, what do cows say?

Baby says, "Moo!"